DODSWORTH IN ROME

Written and illustrated by
TIM EGAN

HOUGHTON MIFFLIN BOOKS FOR CHILDREN
HOUGHTON MIFFLIN HARCOURT
BOSTON NEW YORK 2011

For Chris and Brian,

our incredible sons.

Houghton Mifflin Books for Children is an imprint of
Houghton Mifflin Harcourt Publishing Company.

www.hmhbooks.com

The text of this book is set in Cochin.
The illustrations are ink and watercolor on paper.

Library of Congress Cataloging-in-Publication Data

Egan, Tim.
Dodsworth in Rome / written and illustrated by Tim Egan.
p. cm.
Summary: Dodsworth and his duck companion have a lovely time in
Rome, even thought the duck tries to improve the ceiling of the Sistine
Chapel and takes all the coins from the Trevi Fountain.
ISBN 978-0-547-39006-2
[1. Voyages and travels—Fiction. 2. Rome (Italy)—Fiction. 3. Italy—
Fiction. 4. Ducks—Fiction.] I. Title.
PZ7.E2815Dor 2011
[E]—dc22
2010007024

Manufactured in China
LEO 10 9 8 7 6 5 4 3 2 1

4500265499

CONTENTS

CHAPTER ONE

THE ETERNAL CITY

The sun began to set over Italy.

The train came to a stop.

Dodsworth smiled and looked down at the duck.

"Rome!" he said.

"Okay," said the duck.

The duck started walking away.

"Where are you going?" asked Dodsworth.

"You said roam," said the duck, "so I'm roaming."

"I meant Rome, Italy," said Dodsworth.

"We're here."

The duck paused for a moment.

"I knew that," he said.

"You can't wander off," said Dodsworth.

"Who, me?" said the duck. "Never."

They walked out of the station.

A small red scooter zoomed past.

"That looks like fun," said Dodsworth.

The duck agreed, so they rented a scooter.

They rode through the streets of Rome.

The scooter was very fast.

Many other scooters and cars whizzed by.

They all came really close to each other.

The duck held on tight.

He had to shut his eyes.

"Look!" said Dodsworth. "There's the Coliseum!"

The duck still had his eyes closed.

"Very nice," he said, even though he didn't see it.

A few moments later, Dodsworth shouted, "Wow!
The Pantheon! It's more than two thousand
years old!"

"Great," said the duck, but his eyes were
still shut.

They raced down a few more streets.

"See that?" said Dodsworth. "There's the
Trevi Fountain!"

"Amazing," said the duck, even though, again,
he saw nothing.

"Hey," said Dodsworth, "gelato!
That's Italian ice cream."
The duck finally opened his eyes.
"Ice cream!" he said. "I love ice cream!"
Dodsworth pulled the scooter over
and stopped.

Dodsworth and the duck ordered gelatos.

Dodsworth got a cone with three scoops:

chocolate, vanilla, and strawberry.

The duck got a cone with seven scoops:

hazelnut, spumoni, rum raisin, almond,

pistachio, coffee, and butterscotch.

They watched folks throw coins into the
Trevi Fountain.

"They say if you toss a coin over your shoulder
into the fountain, you'll return to Rome
someday," said Dodsworth.

"Why leave in the first place?" asked the duck.

"Good point," said Dodsworth.

Looking for a place to stay, Dodsworth
drove a little slower this time.
They rode past giant marble statues and stone
fountains and old bridges and lush gardens.
Cathedral bells rang throughout the city.
Dodsworth and the duck loved Rome already.

CHAPTER TWO

THE SISTINE CHAPEL

They found a hotel near Vatican City.

The next day, Dodsworth said, "Let's go to the Sistine Chapel."

"Why?" asked the duck.

"Because Michelangelo painted the ceiling," said Dodsworth.

"What color did he paint it?" asked the duck.

"I'll show you," said Dodsworth.

"I think I'll bring my suitcase," said Dodsworth,

"I feel better having it with me."

They walked to Saint Peter's Square.

There were huge columns all around.

"I feel smaller than usual," said the duck.

"You can say that again," said Dodsworth,

but the duck decided not to.

They followed a group into the Sistine Chapel.

Everyone looked up at the ceiling.

"It's magnificent," said Dodsworth.

"Yeah," said the duck, "not bad."

A few minutes later, the duck said, "That's weird."

"What's weird?" asked Dodsworth.

"There isn't one duck in the entire painting,"

said the duck.

Dodsworth laughed.

"I hadn't noticed," he said.

They walked all around the Vatican.

There were masterpieces everywhere.

"These guys were good," said the duck.

"You can say that again," said Dodsworth.

This time, the duck actually did say it again.

They passed by some workers.

The workers were painting a doorway.

The duck saw a bucket of white paint.

"Perfect," he said.

Dodsworth noticed the duck was missing.

"Now where did he go?" he said.

Dodsworth started back the way they had come in.

"He couldn't have gone far," he said.

Dodsworth walked back into the Sistine Chapel.

He looked around but didn't see the duck.

He looked up.

Dodsworth couldn't believe his eyes.

"STOP!" he shouted at the top of his voice.

The duck was up on the ceiling.

He was holding a brush with white paint.

"I was just going to add a duck," he said.

"Do not move," said Dodsworth.

"Now come down from there."

"You just said not to move," said the duck.

"Come down now," said Dodsworth.

The duck came down.

"This is a masterpiece," said Dodsworth.

"You can't touch it."

"Sorry," said the duck. "I just thought it
needed a duck."

CHAPTER THREE
THE FLEA MARKET

"You have to learn to behave yourself,"
said Dodsworth.

The duck promised.

"Okay, let's find something to eat," said
Dodsworth.

They walked for about a mile.

They saw a huge outdoor market.

"Hey, look," said Dodsworth, "a flea market.

Let's go."

"No, thanks," said the duck. "I don't like fleas."

"It doesn't really have fleas," said Dodsworth.

"It's just called that."

The market was very crowded.

"We should watch out for pickpockets,"
said Dodsworth.

The duck didn't have any pockets.

The duck watched out for fleas instead.

They walked around the market for a
while.
Dodsworth looked at watches and lamps
and books and hats and other things.
The duck just kept looking for fleas.

They stopped at a pizza stand.

They ordered two slices of pepperoni pizza.

Across the way, Dodsworth saw a pizza-throwing contest.

"Ya know," he said to the duck, "you might be great at that. You're good at throwing food."

The duck entered the contest.

He could barely reach the table.

He piled some boxes to stand on.

The duck started throwing the dough.

He threw perfect pizzas.

A crowd started gathering around.

Nobody threw pizzas as well as the duck.

Things seemed to be going quite well until

Dodsworth yelled, "Duck! My suitcase is gone!"

"I bet the fleas took it!" shouted the duck.

"There are no fleas!" yelled Dodsworth. "But we

have to find it!"

The duck jumped up onto the table.

He looked all around the market.

He pointed at a hippo with a suitcase.

"There it is!" he shouted. "And there's the thief!"

Dodsworth ran up to the hippo and grabbed

the case.

"Hey, what's the big idea?" said the hippo.

It was not Dodsworth's case.

"Sorry," said Dodsworth, "my mistake."

The duck spotted a horse with a suitcase.

"There it is!" shouted the duck.

They ran up to the horse, but he wasn't

holding their case either.

Many cases looked just like theirs.

They ran all over the market.

Dodsworth knocked over a fruit stand

by accident.

"That's something I would do," said the duck.

The merchants all stared at Dodsworth.

It wasn't a very good afternoon.

Dodsworth and the duck left the flea market.

"Most of our money was in that case," said

Dodsworth. "I've had that thing for years."

"Rotten pickpockets," said the duck.

All day, they wandered around Rome.

Their suitcase seemed gone for good.

Evening fell over the city.

Dodsworth and the duck were very tired.

"We can't go back to the hotel without money,"

said Dodsworth. "We'll look more in a little bit."

He laid down on the Spanish Steps and

took a nap.

CHAPTER FOUR
ARRIVEDERCI

Dodsworth slept for most of the night.
When he woke up, the duck was counting
money on the steps.
"Where did you get that?" he asked.
"I found it," said the duck.

"Where?" asked Dodsworth.

"Around the corner," said the duck.

"We should find out whose it is," said Dodsworth.

"That would be impossible," said the duck.

Dodsworth wasn't sure what to do.

"I guess it's okay since you just found it,"
said Dodsworth.

"Exactly," said the duck. "Finder's keepers."

"Well, this is good luck!" said Dodsworth.

They celebrated with a delicious breakfast.

They took an afternoon carriage ride
through the city.

They ate ravioli near the Forum.

They had spaghetti that evening at a fine
restaurant. It was a splendid day.

The next day, they strolled along the Tiber
River.

They crossed over the Bridge of Angels.

They had a delicious lunch near the Arch of
Constantine.

That evening, they dined on rigatoni with
tomato sauce.

"I can't believe all that money was just lying
on the ground," said Dodsworth.

"Well, not exactly on the ground," said the duck.

"Oh?" said Dodsworth. "What do you mean,
not exactly?"

"It was in that giant fountain," said the duck.

Dodsworth spit out his rigatoni.

"The Trevi Fountain!?" shouted Dodsworth.

"You took the money from the Trevi Fountain?!"

"Nobody wanted it," said the duck.

"I don't believe this!" said Dodsworth.

"We could get arrested!"

He paid the check and they went outside.

"We have to come up with that money and
return it," said Dodsworth. "It's not ours."
The duck felt bad.
Just then, a small car skidded up next to them.
"Aha!" said the driver. "I found you!"
Dodsworth panicked.

"I can explain!" he said. "The duck didn't understand about the fountain! He does crazy things all the time!"

"That's true," said the duck.

"I don't know what you mean," said the fellow, "but I believe this is yours."

He pointed to the suitcase in the back seat.

Dodsworth was thrilled.

"Where did you find it?" he asked.

"The duck used it to stand on for the pizza
throwing contest," said the fellow.

"Oops," said the duck. "Guess I forgot."

"Also, the duck won the contest," he added.

"You get ten free pizzas at Luigi's!
Congratulations!"

"*Grazie!*" said Dodsworth.

He turned to the duck. "That means 'thank you.'"

"Ahh," said the duck. "Well, hey—grassy, grassy!"

"*Arrivederci!*" said the fellow as he drove away.

"I can't believe you were standing on the
suitcase," said Dodsworth.

"Just wanted to make the trip a little more
exciting," said the duck.

"Well, you did," said Dodsworth, "that you did."

They both laughed and walked down the street.

They arrived at Trevi Fountain.

They turned around and closed their eyes.

And as the bells began to chime throughout

Rome, they slowly started throwing coins into

the water.